Hope of Stones

Hope of Stones

Poems

Anna Elkins

Press 53
Winston-Salem

Press 53, LLC
PO Box 30314
Winston-Salem, NC 27130

First Edition

IMMERSION POETRY SERIES
edited by Christopher Forrest

Author Photo by Howard Romero

Cover design by Christopher Forrest and Kevin Morgan Watson

Library of Congress Control Number
2020933190

Printed on acid-free paper
ISBN 978-1-950413-21-8

To the you in me

Many thanks to the editors of the following journals where versions of these poems first appeared:

Ascent, "The Poet Sings a Hymn for the Burning"

Connecticut River Review, "The Poet Enters the Nun's Castle" & "The Poet Bakes the Nun a Plum *Galette*"

The Cresset, "The Poet Dreams of the Nun & The Architect"

Deep Travel: Souvenirs from the Inner Journey, "The Poet & the Bloodstone"

Palette Poetry, "The Poet to the Nun"

Pedestal 84, "The Poet Enters the Architect's Catacombs"

Prime Number Magazine, "The Architect Dines with Bread & Relics

"The Poet Enters The Architect's Catacombs" & "The Architect Disbelieves" were semifinalists for the Janet B. McCabe Poetry Prize.

This manuscript was a finalist for the Tupelo Press 2019 Dorset Prize, judged by Mary Jo Bang.

Contents

quæ sursum volo videre—I desire to see what is beyond

PROLOGUE

The Nun

The Spanish nun, Saint Teresa of Ávila, lived from 1515 to 1582. After an encounter with God, she wrote *The Interior Castle*, describing the invisible dwellings of our spirits. Teresa founded the Barefoot Carmelite order, wanting a return to simplicity in the Catholic faith. She experienced ecstatic spiritual encounters & wrote about them obliquely—possibly to avoid persecution because of her *converso* family heritage in the Inquisition. Lorenzo Bernini later immortalized one of Teresa's divine encounters in his sculpture of an angel piercing her with a holy arrow. When Teresa died, legend holds that her body did not decay for days & instead gave off the scent of lilies.

The Architect

The French architect, Charles-Axel Guillaumot, lived from 1730 to 1807. He wrote copious pamphlets about architecture over the course of his career, but his greatest achievement remains largely unseen. By consolidating the layers of abandoned quarries beneath Paris, he saved the city from collapsing back into the hollow spaces created to remove the very stone that had built it. After a Parisian cemetery burst its retaining walls, the bones were exhumed & dumped into a section of the quarries Guillaumot named the catacombs. He had the bones stacked in neat orders of femurs & skulls that can still be seen today—in a section comprising only $1/800^{th}$ of the quarry underworld he spent years reinforcing. The rest of that realm lies almost entirely abandoned.

Hope of Stones

PRAY

Nun | nən

1. a woman who belongs   vows   &   &
2. especially one who   prays

The Poet Dreams of The Nun & The Architect

You who never met

who built an invisible castle   who built a hidden city

who left one order   who named one catacomb
to build another   after another

From her Prologue: From his Preface:

"May this account render   "These remarks were intended
him glory and . . . "   to appear . . . "

living stones   dead bones

To build the unseen, remove the rubble

to pave a path   to pillar collapsing streets
to God   from beneath

Holy the stone   Holy the rejection,
the builders rejected   holy the acceptance

Holy the stone   Holy the city
that yields water   without residents

Holy, holy, holy heaven   Holy preserving of earth

Make holy the hope of stones

The Nun to God

Ávila, Spain

La vida es sueño—life is a dream

Forever, I love you.
Forever, you stand
at the gates of the castle
I did not know how to build
but did—with angels & pain.
Take me. Take my heart
& mind & body—all.
They are inviolate, yours.
They are the *tinto vino* of autumn,
when the grapes begin their sweet rot
& farmers scythe the pulse of wheat.
Turn me into Eucharist.
Help me speak your holy language.
Let me hear & understand
the tongues of desire.
I want you, though never
as much as you want me.
Impossible belief!
I cannot pretend to *not*
love this love—
yourself, myself, selfless.
To those who wonder
at *rhema* & days,
say with me to Him:
Be my day. Be my night.
O come to the night!
I'll stand watch
like the guards
on the walls I left
to build a sanctum
free of human hindrance.
Impossible dream!
Be my *paradiso*—
my heaven-on-earth heart.

The Poet to The Nun

Ávila, Spain

In my language, *earth*
is an anagram for *heart*

& angels glean

integrals & triangles.

You left us a spirit
castle, crenelated
with ecstasy.
Did you know
that chemists
have tried to capture
that bliss in a pill?
Strange transmutation.
Like the goal of those
in your time
trying to turn
lead to gold.

I crave your
transverberation.
To be love-pierced,
to be transformed,
to live the madder
alchemies
of communion
& desire

& lighted delight.

The Architect Assumes

Paris, April

Today, I assumed my duties as Inspector of Quarries.
It rained, so I rode a sedan chair to the end of Rue
de Vaugirard. As if to confirm my appointment,
part of the street had just collapsed when I arrived,
leaving a chasm twenty feet across. I stood at the edge
of an urban abyss that smelled of ancient cellars—
a whiff of history. Beneath these deceiving streets
whole hollow pockets of abandoned quarries wait
to collapse. I will halt this. I will rebuild the *cloches*
of rubble to preserve the city that would not accept
me—will give the City of Light the greatest
gift it does not know it needs.

The Poet Asks the Architect

Paris, April

Did you prefer red wine or white?

Or did you think only of the unstable stones
deep beneath the city?

Did you wear your wig far back on your forehead
so you could feel the nearness of a ceiling?

Did you love infrastructure even as a boy?

Did you enjoy your studies in Rome?

Did you love your wife?

Or did you only marry her because she was
the daughter of the chief architect of Paris?

Or was that "only" an *everything?*

Did it surprise you when the street fell in
on the day you began your post?

Did the rain clear when you left that afternoon?

Did you return home beneath a spring sky like
today's—holy blue with cartoon cumulous arcing
over Notre Dame—knowing the bright sun
would never reach the world you would build?

Did you care?

The Poet Writes on the Banks of the Chetco

Siskiyou National Forest, Oregon

I travel the weave of the given.
Hand me a pencil,
cut off my head,
and I will draw you heaven.
                    —Annie Dillard

I wake where we camped on the stony banks
of the mellow river—not far from where
it feeds to the sea. Here, cell reception means
cells receiving peace. Ions & I beside still waters.

Dawn is slow & cold. The forest of firs
lightens by degrees. Fog pulls from branches,
vanishes. Next month, all this will burn
in wildfire & I'll wish I'd sketched it,

but right now, I only know the call of gull
& the sound of someone approaching on stones—
a friend bringing coffee without a word.
In that silence, words can form.

The Nun's Castle

To a young novitiate

*It came to me that the soul is like a castle made
exclusively of diamond or some other very clear crystal. In
this castle are a multitude of dwellings, just as in heaven
there are many mansions.*
—Saint Teresa from *The Interior Castle*

Imagine yourself as a castle.
See, here—
the library of longing,
so stacked with fulfilled love,
you need a ladder
to reach hope.
& here,
the open windows of vision—
infinity mirrors bending you
to distant bliss.
Feel the woven carpet
beneath your feet—
no low magic,
it lifts you to beauty.
Step into the garden
& fill with fountain sound.
Remember splendor
& how you are
its ever-dwelling.
Everything here is a
metaphor for heaven.
You can spend the rest
of your life
entering
& entering
& entering in.

The Poet & the Bloodstone

Ávila, Spain

Today is research day. First, The Nun's museum.
It brims with depictions of heaven speaking
to the saint. In paintings, doves & rays of light
descend & suspend above her upturned face.
Speech ribbons unfurl toward her from angels.
The saint was known to levitate, so I half expect
the painted words to lift from their composition
& twirl about. They stay put.
                                            Next, the *Catedral
de Ávila*. Here, I see the grandeur The Nun left
behind. This church was built with bloodstone—
granite shot through with iron. It looks like
history has bled across the walls. The stone came
from a nearby quarry, & I think of The Architect.
What we pull from the earth & what we do with it.
I sit a long while on a hard pew, but my most
profound thought is how best to get to the train
station tomorrow.
                                Time to search for gazpacho
& *Rioja*—things that *don't* last for centuries. I keep
forgetting that in this country, I'm an outsider
trying to dine before nine.
                                            The Nun founded
her simple convent outside the city walls.
Paris thought The Architect an outsider for not
being born in France. I am always looking
for what lies outside—even dining hours.
                                                        I find
an open café & order wine the color of iron & time.

The Architect Disbelieves

Beneath Rue d'Enfer, Paris

Paris has another Paris under herself, which has its streets,
its intersections, its squares, its dead ends, its arteries
and its circulation.
          —Victor Hugo, *Les Miserables*

There is no weather down here. It's old & warm,
always. The lantern light soaks into stone,
the underworld eating it whole. Every day, I descend
into this second city to save the one built above it.
The heaving & hefting. We turn *cloches* of fallen
rubble into stalagmites of stonework. One worker said
it's as if we're building a cathedral upside down.
For each right-side-up cathedral on the surface,
we mark its spot here below with a *fleur-de-lis*. We
match the tunnels to the streets above & give them
the same names. We leave the spaces beneath houses
to their owners—who own their bit of Paris to the center
of the earth. If they wished, they could dig cellars
to hell. Priests talk about the end of time—how
all this will burn. I can't say why, but I do not
believe them. Meanwhile, people gather in daylight,
in stained-glass masses of stones & hope.

The Poet Picks Plums in the Fire

Oregon, Wildfire Season

Being in a state of mystery seems to be my calling.
—Luci Shaw

The Chetco Bar fire keeps burning. Last I heard,
it was only 5% contained. Yesterday, the air quality
reached hazardous levels, shown in burgundy
on the index—the most dangerous color to date.
This morning, the air is merely unhealthy. I don
my new N-95 mask & drive to pick plums on Beall
Lane. The mask is hard to wear—bands of elastic cut
tight across my cheeks, & it's stuffy inside. I arrive
to the orchard & begin to fill my bags with fruit.
More than once, I pull a plum to my mouth to eat
before remembering the mask.
                                    Shaw once wrote
of harvesting fog—a Peruvian tradition of catching
water from moisture-thick air. A distiller in San
Francisco makes vodka from his city's famous fog.
But even the most ardent, barbecue-loving
man-on-fire wouldn't want to capture this smoke.
A local church invited the Klamath tribe to perform
a rain dance. A friend set out a bowl of water
for the rain fairies.
                        I create a micro-climate,
terrarium-style, inside this mask—making
& harvesting my own, breathy rain.

The Poet Asks The Nun

The daily –*ing* of everything—
eternal present progressive
with a rare, gerund pause.
All of life an –*ing*:

writing, cleaning, helping,
cooking, visiting, traveling,
planning, hoping, sleeping,
eating, dancing, laughing,
hoping, failing, coughing,
stopping, starting, loving.

Your language is free
of the -*ing*. Were you free
of the cycle it implies?

The Nun Wonders

I have not learned to rest
from the never-dones.
From the cycle of days that roll
forward, pull me along,
& knot me into place.
I am locked in chronology
with the linear & the visitors.
Where is the majesty of *kairos*?
Where do time & distance turn
into the fingers of heaven
& tap the surface of earth?
The myth of history.
The fist of effort
to exist within it.

The Architect Dines with Bread & Relics

Today, I ate inside the earth. One of the miners,
a former sailor from Brittany, shared his baguette
& oysters. He smiled & pulled a shell from his coat.
He held it out to me. I took it & turned its whorl
toward the lantern. Smiling, I said, "This is older than
the ones you've shucked for lunch." The man nodded,
"From down here. This was once all water & fish." He
swept his arm in front of us. "& now we bring creatures
of the sea back to what once was sea." I looked up
at the rough ceiling. "& now a city above we keep
from sinking." I looked down at my hands: bread
in one, fossil in the other. Given & lent in bones
of holding. I returned the relic & ate the bread.

The Poet, Fragmented, to the Architect

*The stone that the builders rejected
has become the cornerstone.*
                    —Psalm 118:22

by design or by might

the numbered tunnels

the rumor that a resident could find
his way home beneath the streets better
than on them

how people unknowing
built houses over quarry voids
plotted gardens over underpinnings

if cut stones live longer than words

playing rock paper scissors with

what lasts forever

The Nun Tells the Devil

You've tried before,
& you'll try again.
That is the only faith
I have in you.
It didn't work—
telling the Son of God
you'd turn stones to bread
there in the desert.
It didn't work—
telling me I deserved
fancy fruits & choice meats.
I get my bread
from heaven.
I say this as much
to tell you off
as to remind myself.
Because I see
your sneaky smile
in my own.
He may be within me,
but wherever He is,
you're never far away.
I keep my eyes open.

The Architect Tells of His Collection

Stone fruit are fine tutors.
                    —Jaya Savige

It's become a kind of hobby, these fossils
from the quarries. Seashells but also—& this
sounds strange—what I think to be petrified
fruit. I found one in the shape of a plum.
Paint it purple & it could pass for real
in one of those fancy table settings so *en vogue*.
In fact, I saw one such still life at a fine dinner
last night. The talk after—not so still, not so fine.
Politics are thick these days. A pall forms
amid citizens & sovereigns. I worry about
the shape it will take & how it will harden.

The Poet Listens to Bells & Angels

Mount Angel Abbey, Oregon

The bells have names, which I've forgotten. I woke to them ringing at 5:20. Between the bell tower & my window, a marble angel stands guard in the rain. As I begin to write, the bells begin to ring again. I came here to rest, not work, though later I'll find myself in the curvilinear, mid-century library looking through books on Saint Teresa. When your work is your love, what does rest look like? The guardian angel stands, implacable, in the rain. I write like I'm trying to rest: with no purpose. I see the angel. I hear the bells. Soon, the library will open. Soon, I'll start craving not just food for the soul but food for the body. Maybe I'll eat the kale-beet salad I brought. Maybe I'll walk into town & treat myself to steak. If I could, I'd fill myself with bells. I am learning to live with hunger. The angel watches. Or maybe it listens.

The Nun Covets

There is a time
for penance
& a time
for partridge.
I confess
to gluttonous
hunger
for Spirit.
I ask you
for a thing
I need—
even covet.
A thing not
so much a thing
as a being.
You.
Feed
my holy greed
for more
than a stomach
could crave.
Give me
more of you—
even as I hide
the glory you give
in secrets
or subversions
for fear of being
called a heretic.
I'm willing
to risk it.
Grant me
your self & song
that my life
might sing
with you.
It is time.

The Poet Hungers

Built a fire in the hearth.
Cut my knuckle on kindling.
Wrote a poem smudged with soot.

The fire dies.
The knuckle bleeds.
The poem fails.

Another fire catches,
another poem catches—
both hungry enough to burn.

BUILD

Architect | är-kə-tekt

1. one who designs   &   constructs
2. especially one who   undertakes   to build

The Nun Constructs a Kingdom

O the spiritual alphabet
we use to spell
our lives—to spell
the words we pray
in silence.

O the presumption
to talk to you by ourselves,
to believe we can speak
not just with men
but with angels
& with you.

O the wild thought
that you would touch us,
that we could levitate
in your love—
& say *put me down!*
& you would.

O that you show us
the castle of our spirits—
place of moats & miracles,
corridors & constellations.

O that you help us
long for what
we don't yet know
to long for.

The Poet Enters The Nun's Castle

I.
The plums ripened *while I was beseeching the Beloved.*

II.
I pulled them from the tree, asking it to *give us understanding of the magnitude.*

III.
The tree answered when I bit into its stone fruit: *we are already blessed.*

IV.
Gathering. Pitting. Cutting. Baking into cobblers for friends. Remember: *the important thing is not to think much but to love much.*

V.
What is the hope of every plum & person? *Perfect union.*

VI.
When I was six, I tried to dye the green plums purple. *I wish I could say more about this, but it is ineffable.*

VII.
After the ripening, the first frost. After the frost, the freezer full of plums. *I confess that I am deeply confused.*

The Nun Commissions a Painting

It was the vision
that did it—seeing
you at the pillar,
beaten & bloody,
able to escape
but staying on
for the cross.
When the sister
finished painting it,
I stood transfixed.
I wanted to know
if that *is* the color
of your eyes.
How to say
how glad I am
for such a dark
reminder of your
sacrifice—carrying
the weight of a world
that wouldn't see
it had built its heavy
self on hollowness.
At first glimpse,
the pillar looks
stronger than you.
But even at your most
broken,
you pillared
the universe.
Death for life—
you teach me the art.

The Poet Paints

Pentimento: *A visible trace of earlier painting*
beneath a layer or layers of paint on a canvas

or on a sheet of paper, or on a life.
Today, I paint for the mystics.

But no realism here—no canvas
equivalent of Bernini's marble.

I set my easel on the deck so the paint
can drip & drip & drip.

I wait for each swath to dry—
can't rush, else a mess.

Ten layers & an afternoon later,
a world of acrylic stalactites

is born. Some of the thin columns
suspend. Some link above

with below. Some disappear.
See here, see here, they say. Or:

See. Hear. See what you leave & what
you reach for. Hear what will come.

The Architect & the Ossuary

The Cimitière des Saints Innocents has finally met
its own end. Nearby residents found decomposing
corpses in their cellars. That after the neighborhood
milk had been souring in the foul air. Almost
a millennium of bodies have festered within those
retaining walls. Which poor corpse caused the break?
I proposed to transport the graveyard bones to one
of the consolidated quarries. In cosmic humor,
the entrance is at the Street of Hell. The displaced
dead will have new homes in three subterranean acres.
I call this place the catacombs, in memory of those
in Rome—the city that *did* accept me. Proud Paris
now rumbles with wagonloads of her citizen
skeletons. The night streets ring with chanting priests.
Everything smells of death & incense. Other
cemeteries will be emptied here. It could take years
to transport the millions who will call this realm
home. Perhaps I, too, will lie here someday
& Paris will finally call me her own.

The Poet Enters The Architect's Catacombs

Somewhere beneath the former Rue d'Enfer, Paris

at a depth of 12 to 13 fathoms, it's core-quiet down here

pieces of stone lifted by hand now lift the earth up from
within herself, held with mortar of bones

The memory of excavations is almost fragrant   The ceiling
above me once collapsed into a tumble
of *voussoirs*—no single keystone to speak of—& this

without making anyone the least bit nervous, though I move
away fast   Bodies know

much more must and can be done to remedy all the damages here
Everywhere   Did you know,

in the void of the quarry, smoke can linger for hours

One can suspend the scent of perfume, too   This
distracts me from the fear of being crushed
alive   Or crushed to death

It had to be resolved, this descent   One stair at a time
      One corridor after another & a final glimpse
up a shaft to see the pinhole light of sky   shining
through a manhole cover   too far above

The Nun on *Nones* & Naughts

Will any of the petitions
& papers, the work & women—
will any of it or us matter?
I don't wish to be remembered.
I do wish for faith to last—free
of frippery, devoted
to the most whole love
we cracked cups can muster.
If all for naught?
I continue anyway.
Midday, I pray the *none*—
that none of this be wasted.

The Architect & the Macabre

Thousands of carts of bones, of earth, of coffin
wood. Hundreds of torches & ells of canvas.
Dozens of pounds of candles & solder. One
goal: to empty the cemeteries. This collection
of skeletons will be unsurpassed. At Montrouge,
we dump the bones into a hole, & a dangling
chain scatters them as they fall. At the bottom,
we arrange them in columns & rows, creating
friezes of femurs & walls of skulls. Bones of third-
century saints—those who died before Saint Denis
Christianized the city—mix with bones of those
I might have known. Epochs & generations
blend, no origin left to matter.

The Poet to the Architect

Things I continue to marvel at:

The number of the Parisian dead you interred—
in their many pieces—was ten times more than
the number of Parisians living at the time.

Only one-eight-hundredth of your subterranean
palace is open to the public.

Almost no one knows who you are, & most credit
for the catacombs goes to your successor,
Héricart de Thury, a more marketable man.

Your ossuary is the most egalitarian place in Paris:
Pascal & Robespierre, nuns & prostitutes, killed
& killers—all *tête-à-tête* (or skull-to-skull) for eternity.

Each part of the body continues to dispossess
the darkness.

You made art of death.

The Nun, Dreaming

Each night I gaze
at the painting
from my childhood
& pray you give me
such water as lives there.
That my dreams
might flow with you.
That I might drink you in
& spill you out.
I wait, content
while contending,
building rough aqueducts
to the Source
while still believing
in the possible
architecture of rest.
I try to become brilliant
at receiving your love.
I try to move
from *I do* to *I am*—
to your I-Am-ness.

The Architect, Listing

It is an underground city, with its streets, crossroads
and squares. . . . Cavities, half-broken ceilings, subsidences
that have not yet reached the surface, pillars that have
collapsed . . . what a list. And one eats, drinks and sleeps
in the edifices resting on this precarious crust.
        —Louis-Sébastien Mercier from *Tableau de Paris*

My list is long: draw up plans of quarries, consolidate
the rubble beneath all roads & public spaces, create
service galleries, convince land owners to handle what's
beneath their own houses & keep watch on everything
up to a league from the outskirts of Paris—& that's just
what I signed on for. Now, I have another problem
to address. A *fonti* some twenty meters in diameter
opened up, swallowing part of the aqueduct that feeds
the fountains of Luxembourg Gardens. We must
rebuild 150 meters of it. We are lining Paris, else she list
& cave & crumble. I only hope these labors will last.

The Poet, Fasting

I haven't fasted in years, but I just had a gum graft,
so it's me & juice. I remember the lethargy, the small
headaches of the first two days. Then the third-day
clarity. This is day two—the trough. I let myself rest.
I lie beneath the maple tree on a quilt & watch
the sky between branches.
                  Dull thoughts unspool
up into the trees: how all these leaves will need
raking come fall, what to juice for second breakfast,
when to run the dishwasher.
              Evelyn Underhill
believed that women mystics with worldly tasks
became visionaries & prophets because they could
balance practicalities with transcendence. Goals.
I practice:
         Practicality—I found a recipe for chilled
beet-plum soup. I anticipate both eating it & finding
another purpose for my plums.
               Transcendence—
I am the woman lying beneath the tree & the woman
floating above it, hoping to see God.

The Nun at Her Table

I write, striving to shape
an uncluttered love—
simple & strong, like a table
built by the Son of God
when He walked the earth.
If I could choose
from all relics to venerate,
more than a crown forced
on His head, I'd choose
a wooden chip
of His workmanship.
All things of earth
will pass away.
But I'd like to think
any piece He built
could pass, unburned,
through the end
of time.

The Architect Imprisoned

Versailles, The French Revolution

That my rival designed it is perhaps the worst part
of this prison—in all its decadent excess. While he
concocted a great aerie for pleasure, I toiled beneath
the earth to preserve. Now, because of my royal
appointment & assorted slanders & schemes,
I am banished to elegance. I could laugh.
I think of the monks & nuns who locked themselves
into religion—who chose to live in cells. Such richness
would surely offend them. In this pastel palace, each
golden filigree & flourish is a slap to my dark work.
The place is pocked with *fleurs-de-lis*—
symbols that now only blossom with loss.

The Nun Makes Way

vía purgativa
Beginning
is a sweet hell—
vía, vía, vía.
The way. Through.
The way through
mud & mess,
hobbles & hurries.

vía iluminativa
Progressing
not so much I
toward it,
but it toward me.
Will I open the window
beyond my reach?
vía, vía, vía.

vía unitiva
Uniting
vía prayers
vía dreams
vía you.

The Poet Destroys

Jacksonville, Oregon

The hornets built a nest
in the eave high above
my deck. From their bouquet
of danger, they dive at me

all day. Before dawn,
I plan an ambush
in my nightdress: I open
the ladder, grab

a broom by its bristles,
& climb. I aim the hard
handle toward the dark truss.
Balanced on a rung,

I think of my grandfathers,
both carpenters.
How many hours they must
have spent on ladders,

building places for people
to live & love. I knock
down the nest—
send it flying.

The Architect Dreams of Saint Peter

May it be said of me that I *have tasted that the Lord is good*

May I *come to him, a living stone rejected by men but in the sight of God chosen and precious*

May I, too, be *like living stones . . . built up as a spiritual house*

May I understand what it is *to be a holy priesthood*

May I hear, *"Behold, I am laying in Zion a stone . . ."*

May I recognize *the cornerstone chosen and precious*

May I believe & *"not be put to shame"*

May I call out: *"The stone that the builders rejected has become the cornerstone"*

May I drop this *"stone of stumbling, and . . . rock of offense"*

May I not *stumble*

The Poet Housesits

A Solar Eclipse, Oregon

On the deck, I wait for the sun to crest
the mountains. A fire burns near
Grizzly Peak, & a low bank of smoke
fills the valleys. I don the certified
viewing glasses & wait for my shadow
to disappear from this page.
But I'm not in the path of totality,
& with the smoky skies, I don't
think I'd know an eclipse
was happening. A bit of darking.
The hummingbirds swarm
the hanging feeder, a dozen
at once, as if their world
is ending. JPR plays Pink Floyd
from *Dark Side of the Moon.*
The shadow of my hand is dim
& then isn't. The eclipse fades.
Then, across invisible radio waves,
"Here Comes the Sun."

The Nun Mulls

When the world is too dark

the miry bog

I break the bread & drink the wine—
glad for the

new song in my mouth.

When the problem is too large,
I ask to hear you. You

have given me an open ear.

I may understand by not
understanding.

*I have told the glad news of
deliverance.*

May this union remain though

*evils have encompassed me
beyond number.*

May this prayer do no harm.

*I have not concealed your
steadfast love.*

When

my heart fails me

May I look to you

Aha, Aha!

The Poet Sings a Hymn for Burning

To the cheatgrass,
that grows & dries fast,
& fuels wildfire.
Scent of sun-baked pinecones

To the ferns coming after a burn,
that love the stripped,
mineral soil.
Whiff of summer-hot loam

Smell the refrain of the last blazes
& the ones who helped the land burn
& the ones who helped the land after.
Damp smell of duality

Stand still long enough
& wear the perfume of future fires—
the sad & the necessary.
Scorch of life, searing

Catch the sweet reek of seeds
waiting in cones & those
who know how to start a new world.
Sing the balm of death & life.

The Architect, Unknowing

Still imprisoned in Versailles

Clay & gypsum. I hold my hand to a wall smothered
in panels & tapestries. *Marl & gravel marl.* I wonder
if I miss Paris more than my wife. *Sand & Sandstone.*
Paris—Lutetia, swamp turned city. *Cliquart
& liais.* What have we pulled from you? *Chalk &
plaster.* Above me a chandelier & its crystals where
I want the sky of quarry roof. *Millstone, limestone,
stone.* The tunnel mouths, the unpretending earth.

The Nun to Her Confessor

*[W]hen he established the fountains of the deep, when
he assigned to the sea its limit . . . when he marked out the
foundations of the earth, then I was beside him, like a
master workman. . . .*
—Lady Wisdom,
Proverbs 8:28b-29

Before, prayer was like building
an aqueduct—hauling stones
& designing for flow
from the deep things.
Now, my prayer
is like sitting at a fountain
that fills without me.
Now, my prayer
is not for more but for
the capacity to hold
more of God.
Now, I can implode those
old stones of effort—
can watch them crumble
& collapse. This I know:
when prayer changes
from work to rest,
the answer becomes nothing
less than everything.

The Poet Walks the Walls of Ávila

I pause on the ramparts & listen
to wind. Through crenellations,

you can see for hundreds of years—
or at least to The Nun's convent.

Think of it—all those *monjas* who
married Jesus could call Mary

their mother-in-law—author
of the *Magnificat*. A poet in the family.

Here on the walls, this Poet plays
with Spanish anagrams:

tierra/retira—the earth retires
liceo/cielo—the school of heaven.

God spoke to The Nun
in the casual *you*—*tu* instead of *usted*.

O to hear Mary call her Son by name.
O to hear Him call me by mine.

WONDER

Poet | pō-ət

1. one who writes   makes
2. especially one who

                                        wonders

The Poet Descends Into the Quarries

I. How I Remember the Darkness

This time, it's not the catacombs—the fraction of quarries open to the public, splashy with stacked bones. This time, it's the abandoned realm. It took me several months & emails to arrange this tour, & I asked a friend to join me.

We meet Gilles in a boiler room off a hospital. He unlocks a metal door & leads us down dank, stone steps. Down & down & down. It gets warm & humid. I pull off my coat. As we descend, he gives us history & facts. I scrawl in my notebook, its pages curling. We reach a kind of room with low, rough ceilings. Electric lights hang far apart. Gilles unfolds an old map, wanting to find something he never reveals.

He leads us into & out of tunnels, past pillars & piles of rock. My friend finds a chocolate Easter egg wrapped in gold foil sitting on shoulder-high rubble. Gilles tells her she can keep it. She finds several more over the next hours—shiny mysteries amid stones carved with The Architect's initials, fountains with mirror-still water, & street signs matching those aboveground. I write until my words turn to inky illegibility.

Time suspends. If anything happened to Gilles, we would have no idea how to get back to the surface.

Of a sudden, voices. We emerge from a tunnel into a domed room that could be an etching of a Victorian tableau: around a long table sit a dozen Parisians—the Capuchin Quarry Society taking their two-hour Saturday luncheon. When they see us, they raise their arms & say a chorus of *bonjours* across a tablecloth covered with bottles of wine & lengths of baguette & heaps of cheese & candlesticks with dripping tapers.

I almost trip over a pair of pet food bowls before I see a small, black dog sniffing my boots. Cigarette smoke hangs in visible curls & clouds. Gilles waves his map at the wisps, says the smell can hang in the air for hours. Perfume, too. He tucks the map into his pocket, & with that, the tour ends. He leads us back to the stories of stairs.

Before we reach the locked door at the top, I remember it was said that when The Nun died, her body gave off the scent of lilies for days. I tuck my notebook in my bag & pull on my coat to face the cold above. I rewrap my scarf & the faint scent of a Channel perfume sample awakens. How long might the fragrance of The Nun's life have lingered here?

II. Notes from a Tour with a *cataphile*

200 kilometers of corridors

60 meters below street level

80 to 90% humidity

1720: First street signs used in Paris

1779: The Architect matched signs of quarry streets
to those above

1777: Oldest date engraved down here

1792: France changed its calendar

3R: Third year of the Revolution

Fleurs-de-lis scratched out during the Revolution—
only ten remain

fontis: collapsed sink holes

fonti + vault = something long ago collapsed

a monastery once above, now a hospital

arrows made with candlelight smoke indicate exits

scent of cigarette & sound of laughter

The Architect Wonders

Saint-Pierre de Montmartre, Paris

Aunque es de noche—Although it is night

I am now free to go where I wish, but I wish
for nothing. This evening, no destination
in mind, I found myself in Montmartre, in front
of the sad batterment of Saint Peter's. I stood
as if in mourning—all those mined stones torn
down. I confess I never liked Peter. One minute
he was the rock on which God would build
his Church & the next, the devil was on his back.
But I've come to sympathize with him—or with
the structure that bears his name. Or with all
our human vacillations. I've always wondered
what God was thinking, choosing such weak fools
for his work. All of us, such weak fools. I begin
to think that heaven's building materials
are nothing like the ones we choose to use.

The Poet Hunts for Angels

Saint-Pierre de Montmartre, Paris

I'm not Catholic, but I've come to Easter mass at Saint
Peter's. It's one of the oldest churches in the city, though
part of it was destroyed in the Revolution. Tear-down-
build-up-tear-down—if only that meant building muscles
of love.

      The year The Architect was freed from Versailles,
the last abbess of the convent here was killed by
guillotine. Today, a luckier woman stands between
the choir & the crossing. She sings into a microphone
until the speakers crackle & die. She keeps singing
a capella. The pews fill with people & praise.

           The singer
invites us to sing. I don't know the words, so I look
for depictions of angels. Another poet told me not
to write of angels—too precious, she thought. I wish
she could see the warriors who've guarded my dreams,
whose portraits I've painted. They wield fierce good with
quivers full of selfless prayer—the hardest kind.

           A priest
walks down the aisle & dashes us with holy water.
Incense, beseeching. I don't know that we're giving
the angels anything to work with. The church is packed
now. I give up my seat to a father who sits his toddler
on his lap. I move to the back of the nave, planning to
leave before communion.

          I scan the statuary & stained
glass. Still no angels from where I stand. But I know
they're here, if weary.

           What if we started with heaven
& pulled it to earth?

The Nun Takes a Chance

Prepare for heresy.
On the stairs,
a child appeared to me.
He asked my name.
I said, "Teresa of Jesus.
& what is yours?"
He said, "Jesus of Teresa."
Now I am forever
hovering
between stories,
between realms.
Forever standing
on the landing
of love.

The Poet Bakes The Nun a Plum *Galette*

*These are the facts of the imagination, the very
positive facts of the imaginary world.*
—Gaston Bachelard, *The Poetics of Space*

Dear nun who loved cooking & eating &
believed God also lives among the pots & pans:
I cordially invite you to tea. Can you accept?
My doubt's not for how far the travel—oceans
& centuries are relative—but more for your
cloistered life. Still, you're fully spirit now, so
maybe you can come. I'm making something
lovely with plums. I keep my freezer full of
them—pitted, halved, ready. O the way crust
meets fleshy body of baked fruit. The magic of
it: this is the only plum *galette* that will ever be
made with these plums on this day by these hands
lifting in pastry-dusted praise. & I'd guess this
to be the only plum *galette* ever offered to you
from the close & distant future.

The Poet Writes in Ash

Morning in Oregon

I am thankful for distance—wildfires still far
enough away that my house is safe, though my
shirt smells like campfire & the horizon is an
orange fury. But am I complacent or grateful? I
work with what I've got. Can't fix everything,
just the things within my reach—clean the house,
donate to the wildland firefighters, keep the cat
in at night so he won't go looking for a fight.
People *are* looking for a fight, but the fire started
with lightning. It's no one's fault & blame is lazy.
The worst destruction on our street this year?
The neighbor ripped out the blackberries I've
enjoyed for years. That old annoyance pales in
the smoke. All the losses—large & little. I remind
myself: the cat was born with claws. Blackberries
are non-native & invasive, & aren't we all? Our
best attempts at legacy fail: Carmelite nuns claim
to be tortured by their mother superior, & around
ten sinkholes still appear in Paris each year. Yet
this winter, snow will cover the burned land in
brief forgiveness. Outside right now, the air is
hard to breathe. I spell "hope" in the ash gathered
on the windowsill. I pack a go-bag & lock it in
the trunk of my car.

The Architect Returns

The cycle of a revolution ends & I begin again
my work in the quarries. Things below are much
the same, though the purgers of royalty scratched
out the *fleurs-de-lis* like they scathed the churches
they symbolized. What has changed is how
I decipher darkness. Perhaps this is why I've also
accepted the directorship of the Gobelins Tapestry
Factory. I live in contrast between the bright rooms
of looms & the cavernous opacity of earth, my eyes
always adjusting to the back & forth, the up & down.
I'd like to think I can see a bit better now. That I can
stand at the *bouches de cavage* & trust the tunnels to lead
into the dark—but also back into the light.

The Poet Travels the Weave of the Given

The Lady & the Unicorn: *À mon seul désir*
Cluny Museum, Paris

Perhaps poetry is another of science's deepest
roots: the capacity to see beyond the visible.
—Carlo Rovelli

Touch, taste, smell, hearing, sight.
The five senses hang as five tapestries,
warming stone walls. Each scene blooms
with *mille-fleurs* in gardens of thread.
But it's the fabric of the sixth sense I want
to touch, taste, smell, & hear: *mon seul désir.*

I can only see it & ask—what *is* my sole desire?
More & more I want less & less. I sit & wait
for the lady or the unicorn to reveal what she
or he might mean. Scholars have argued about it,
though they tend to agree on the blending
of secular & sacred, real & imagined.

The museum is about to close. I head out
for the Luxembourg Gardens, crossing
gravel paths, pausing at fountains. Parisians lean
back in green metal chairs, faces to sun,
eyes closed. When The Architect lived,
the tapestries lay forgotten in a faraway castle,

but what if he *did* see the lady & the unicorn?
I pass a café where I once sat with a friend. What if
I sat there with The Nun & ordered us a *tarte tatin*—
which I'd pronounce terribly, but which would
come with a side of cream &, while sharing
the sweetness, we'd listen for secret things?

The Architect Prays for His Daughter

I pray for you a world that won't collapse. A world
secure enough to create in. At first, I wanted to save
this city to prove to it my worth—vanity of young
men. Now, I watch you love a man with his own
pride of proving & cannot fault him. But I can
recommend this: sit at a loom for even half a day.
Watch how long a single line of a grand design can
take. Remember that everything we do will be nothing
more than several threads in the tapestry of time—
small but useful beauty. I no longer care to prove,
& only now do I see that no one asked me to.

The Poet's Work

Manufacture des Gobelins, Paris

Many Theresas [sic] *have been born who found for themselves
no epic life wherein there was a constant unfolding of far-resonant
action; perhaps only a life of mistakes, the offspring of a certain
spiritual grandeur ill-matched with the meanness of opportunity;
perhaps a tragic failure which found no sacred poet and sank
unwept into oblivion.*
—George Eliot, from the Prelude to *Middlemarch*

I wait outside the gates for the Gobelins Tapestry
Factory to open. It's my last day of research in the city,
& I am annoyed at the Metro & the disdain
of the young waiter at lunch. I feel mundane, so
I bought a single souvenir in the Marais—a tiny gold
ring, thread-thin. Silly purchase, just too small for my
right ring finger. Only in this cold does it fit.
                                        No sign
of anyone yet. I want to see where The Architect spent
his second career as director of this factory, where
artisans used their hands until their fingers surely bent.
I hold out my hands—
                        Is someone coming?
                                        No.
The Nun's most grisly relic: her right ring finger. Gray
& shriveled in the museum vitrine, it bore the ring she
used to marry Jesus & was displayed as if sprouting
a feather, with no explanation.
                            Back home, jewelers
promote a woman's right ring finger as the place
to show independence. The left is encircled with
husbands or nothing.
                I wear no pledge to self or man.
No explanation.
                Finally, a guard walks toward the gate,
a ring of golden keys in her hand.
                            In the sound of their
clattering comes a truncated wonder: *How we pull metals
from the earth. How we carve, cut, forge, & shape.*
                                        I move
the new ring to my pinky. It's looser there—easy to
lose. Before I return home, I'll dream I break it.

The Nun's Jewelwork

With this ring,
I pledged myself
to you,
wed myself
to you.
With this ring,
my finger daily
tells my hand—
tells my heart—
whose I am.
With this ring,
I surrender
the silly
myth of rights
to anyone
or anything but
big Love.

The Architect's Crewelwork

Directing a tapestry factory, I've learned all manner
of threads & designs & fabrics. Work I once
thought only for women in parlors I begin
to fathom. The other day, I admired a bit
of crewelwork your mother had set on the table—
tiny flowers formed of linen stitches. In the past,
I'd have simply set my glass on it. Today,
I used the bottom of my glass to magnify the work.
Was the world's first stitch made to link? A ligature?
I suppose design came later—along with the thought
to make a flower bloom forever. Simple as red thread,
fingers, needles. Simple as knowing nothing
is forever but wanting to be wrong.

The Poet Wonders

Oregon, October

The more I wonder, the more I love.
—Alice Walker

It is no longer the month of April & maybes.
It's October & root vegetables—the soil-
pulled concretions of harvest. What we seeded
in spring has grown up & down & waits
for us to lift it from the skin of earth.

How silent prayer was revelation & heresy.

The clouds roll in. The leaves redden.
The cat's coat thickens. We gather
the tangible close & prepare for cold.

How physics is the science of prayer.

One friend is dying. Another is trying to love
someone who doesn't love her back.

I visit the first friend, & we sit on his deck
watching tractors in the adjacent forest dig
foundations for new houses he will never see.

I visit the other friend & notice the old
potatoes she keeps on a shelf. They've
shriveled a bit but have new eyes—new shoots
already looking for somewhere else to grow.

How a perennial can inspire prayer.

The Poet in the Current

Gihon River, Another Autumn

*Now I think there is only one subject worth
my attention and that is the precognition of
the spiritual side of the world and, within
this recognition, the condition of my own
spiritual state.*
                    —Mary Oliver, from *Upstream*

This river flows from Eden,
Vermont. I watch it
out my studio window.

Halfway through my time here,
half the trees have shed
their leaves. I am hinged
between what came
& what comes—
as always.

Last week, it was warm enough
to swim. I walked along
the shore, found a curve
& gravel strand
& stepped in to a cold
that seized my legs & lungs.
I swam upstream—
the current perfect
for staying in place
if you faced it.
Floating leaves nicked
my chin in bright surprise.

Today, it snows—
I feel again the knowing
of the river.
If I surrender to the water,
I will truly move.
If I'm not careful—
or if I am—it will carry
me with promise.

How to Save From Collapse

A Soul

Excavation: Begin by ridding the soul
of the self's clutter.

Masonry: Build a discipline
of daily prayer.

Cartography: Leave a record of divine
visitations & revelations for those
who follow—more intimate than you
ever thought God could be.

A Desire

Excavation: Accept an invitation to dig
through history.

Masonry: Build a passage of imagination
among centuries.

Cartography: Plot a heart of possibility—
more chanced than anything you
thought you wanted.

A City

Excavation: Begin by removing the rubble
from the quarries.

Masonry: Use the excavated stone to build
pillars reinforcing the ceiling of street.

Cartography: Craft a map of that parallel place,
a map on a scale of 1:216—more detailed
than any ever drawn for the city above.

We Build a Kaleidoscope

The word *technology* comes from the Greek words *techne* & *logos*. *Teche* means art, skill, craft, or a system of making. *Logos* means word, utterance, or expression. In that light, technology can be defined as the expression of making.

I.

It begins with a vision—a crystal castle we can fit in our hands. Faceted turrets & crenellations. An architecture of solid certainties. Flawless, but too small to admit entry. Tired of it, we hold the castle out to God, saying, "Here, go ahead & smash it." We look away, waiting for breakage. He accepts our brittle gift. Silence. We wait, turn.

II.

they lift the crystals

                    from their rigid fixing

each clear piece slips free

            hovers in the space   between us

        s   p i n s   s l o w

        light refracts   changes our shapes

the pieces   take on colors

                        fit any person or circumstance

            & morph

        into the eye piece
                        of a kaleidoscope

                we trade judgment for wonder

                    when they turn the handle

                mirrors reflect a world

                        we've never seen

                    they hold

            the miracle

                            out to us

                            we reach for it

EPILOGUE

The Nun

After reforming the Carmelite order, Saint Teresa of Ávila also founded seventeen convents & almost as many cloisters for monks. Before she died, she said to God: "It is time for us to meet one another." She was canonized in 1622 & was the first woman in history to be distinguished as a Doctor of the Church. Her search for union with God continues to inspire generations of mystics. Her life & work illuminate the architecture of spirit.

The Architect

Charles-Axel Guillaumot constructed the largest architectural project in Europe. If the underground galleries of Paris were laid end to end, they would stretch 200 miles. In 2017, a plaza near the catacomb entrance was named for him: Esplanade Charles-Axel Guillaumot. He is still helping Paris from collapsing; his own bones are buried in the quarries, forming walls that support the city.

With love to Notre Dame de Paris
& to rebuilding what has burned

Acknowledgments

My university art professor, Neil Jussila, who taught me to see beyond

Poets Jim Peterson & Tami Haaland, for your wise eyes & hearts

Ersellia Ferron for introducing me to *The Interior Castle*

The Little Free Library on Anderson Creek Road, where I "met" The Architect in a history book & the homes up the hill where I housesat & wrote.

My fellow "Literary Avengers" & Paris *flâneuses*, Christina Ammon & Erin Byrne

The Squaw Valley Community of Writers Poetry Workshop, where the seed for this collection began to germinate

The Glen Workshop, especially Gina Franco & my fellow workshop participants for reading the very first of these poems

Saint Teresa's museums & convent in Ávila, Spain

Mount Angel Abbey, Saint Benedict, Oregon

The Capuchin Society, especially *cataphile* Gilles Thomas

The Catacombs of Paris

Amy Calkins, Anne Waldman, & the brief writing group of Jacksonville, who saw many of these poems as they developed & helped me see them better

Jodi Gladding, who graciously translated several sections of The Architect's pamphlets

The Vermont Studio Center for being a writers' haven & all those who helped get me there, especially Janet & Terry Keating

Sebastian Matthews & Julie Brooks Barbour, the first poets to read this book in its entirety & offer most helpful feedback

Rebel Heart Books & the "Shut Up & Write" group where I made final revisions

Christopher Forrest & Kevin Morgan Watson of Press 53 for giving *Hope of Stones* a wonderful home

Everyone at "Elkinsville," always

Notes

Page 25: Italicized lines in "The Poet Enters the Nun's Castle" from *The Interior Castle* by St. Teresa of Ávila. Translation by Mirabai Starr (Riverhead Books, 2003).

Page 29: Italicized lines in "The Poet Enters the Architect's Catacombs" from *Mémoire sur les Travaux Ordonn. Imprimeur-Librarie* by Charles-Axel Guillaumot (Collège d'Harcourt, Rue de la Harpe. XIII. Paris, 1804). Translation of phrases by Jody Gladding.

Page 40: Italicized lines in "The Architect Dreams of Saint Peter" from 1 Peter.*

Page 42: Italicized lines in "The Nun Mulls" from Psalm 40.*

*All quoted Scripture taken from *The ESV Bible* (The Holy Bible, English Standard Version, Crossway 2001)

Glossary:

bouches de cavage: tunneling mouths

cataphile: catacomb lover (literally: a lover of the below)

cloche: a dome-shaped cover

ell: a measuring unit roughly the length of an arm from the middle finger to the elbow

fleur-de-lis/fleurs-de-lis: symbol of stylized lily/lilies that had once been associated with Catholic saints but later became conflated with French monarchy

fonti/fontis: subsidence cavity/cavities—a bell-shaped cavity left behind when a quarry collapses

monja: nun, sister

rhema: the spoken word of God

subsidence: the gradual or sudden downward sinking of an area of land—a vertical, not horizontal settling

tinto vino: red wine

transverberation: spiritual ecstasy, piercing of divine love

voussoirs: wedge-shaped stones used to construct arches

Bibliography:

Angels of Paris: An Architectural Tour through the History of Paris. Rosemary Flannery. The Little Book Room. 2012.

Art & Physics. Leonard Shlain. Harper Perennial. 2007.

The Book of Her Life. Teresa of Ávila. Translation by Kieran Kavanaugh & Otilio Rodriguez. Hackett. 2008.

Harvesting Fog. Luci Shaw. Pinyon. 2010.

A Little Book on Form, Robert Hass. Ecco. 2017.

Les Miserables. Victor Hugo. Signet Classics. 1995.

Negotiating the Doing-to-Being Boundary. Charlie Sattgast. Bethel Seminary. 2015.

Notebooks of the Mind: Explorations of Thinking. Vera John-Steiner. Oxford University Press. 1997.

On Being Podcast with Krista Tippett. Krista Tippett Public Productions.

The Order of Time. Carlo Rovelli. Riverhead. 2018.

Parisians: An Adventure History of Paris, Graham Robb. Picador. 2011.

The Poetics of Space. Gaston Bachelard. Penguin. 2014.

"Magnifera." Jaya Savige. *Poetry.* Vol. CCVIII, Number 2. May 2016. 116.

Les rues de Paris au XVIIIe siécle: le regard de Louis Sébastien Mercier. Elisabeth Bourguinat. Paris Musées. 1999.

The Separate Notebooks. Czeslaw Milosz. Translated by Robert Hass & Robert Pinsky. Ecco. 1984.

The St. Teresa of Avila Prayer Book. Vinita Hampton Wright. Paraclete Press. 2015.

Teresa of Avila: The Progress of a Soul, Cathleen Medwick. Knopf. 1999.

Tickets for a Prayer Wheel, Annie Dillard. Bantam. 1974.

An Underground World: The Catacombs of Paris. Sylvie Robin, Jean-Pierre Gély, Marc Viré. Paris Musées. 2013.

Upstream. Mary Oliver. Penguin. 2016.

Untold Sisters: Hispanic Nuns in Their own Words, Electa Arenal & Stacey Schlau. University of New Mexico Press. 1989.

View with a Grain of Sand. Wisława Szymborska. Translated by Stanisław Barańczak & Clare Cavanagh. Harcourt Inc. 1995.

Anna Elkins is a traveling poet and painter. She earned a BA in English and art, and an MFA and Fulbright Fellowship in poetry. She has written, painted, and taught on six continents— publishing her writing and exhibiting her art along the way. She has illustrated books by others and authored several books of her own. Anna also teaches classes in the crossroads of art + word + spirit, and one of her greatest joys is encouraging people to discover and delve into their creativity. Learn more at www.annaelkins.com

CPSIA information can be obtained
at www.ICGtesting.com
Printed in the USA
BVHW030918020420
576644BV00001B/21